Enid Blyton ™

The Spelling Spell

Illustrated by Pam Storey

Once Mr Stamp-About went through Dimity Wood in a great rage. He stamped as he went and muttered to himself and he even shook his fist in the air.

"I'll pay old Snorty back for not giving me what he owes me! How am I to pay my bills if he doesn't pay his? How dare he say that the apples I sold him were bad and not worth a penny! How dare he not pay me for them!"

The rabbits ran away from his stamping feet and the squirrels bounded up into the trees. The robin followed him, flying from tree to tree in wonder. What was the matter now with noisy old Stamp-About?

Stamp-About didn't notice that he had taken the wrong path in the wood. He went on and on, and then suddenly found that the path was getting very narrow. He stopped and looked round.

"I've taken the wrong path! All because of Snorty! I am so angry with him that I don't even see the way I am walking!"

He stood there a few moments, wondering what to do. "Perhaps there's someone nearby who will hear me if I shout and tell me the right path," he thought. So he gave a loud shout. "Ho there! I want help!"

Nobody answered at all, and the birds all flew away in fright, for Stamp-About had such a tremendous voice! He yelled again. "Ho there! I want help!"

And this time a voice called back to him – a very cross voice indeed.

"Will you be quiet? You're spoiling my spell!"

Stamp-About could hardly believe his ears. Spoiling someone's spell? Whose? And if the someone was near enough to shout back, why didn't he come to help Stamp-About? "Rude fellow!" thought Stamp-About, angrily. "I'll go and tell him what I think of him!"

So he pushed his way fiercely through the bushes and came to a little clearing, set neatly round with red-spotted toadstools in a ring. In the middle sat a little fellow in a long black cloak that shimmered like moonlight. He had two long feelers on his forehead, just like a butterfly.

In front of him a small fire burnt and on it was a bowl of clear glass which, strangely enough, seemed not to mind the flames at all.

"Why didn't you come to help me?" stormed Stamp-About.

"Please go away," said the little fellow, turning round. "Yelling like that in my spell time, I never heard of such a thing! Go and buy yourself a few manners!"

Stamp-About almost exploded with temper. "How dare you," he cried. "Who are you, you miserable, uncivil little fellow?"

"I'm Weeny, the little wizard," said the small man. "And I get my living by making spells at this time each day and selling them. And then you come blustering along and spoil them all. Just when I was making gold, too! Pah!"

"Gold?" said Stamp-About, in quite a different voice. "Good gracious – can you make gold?"

"Not exactly," said the little wizard. "But my spells can! I've only to pop the right things into my little glass bowl here and spell each one as they dissolve – and at the end what do I find? A handful of gold at the bottom of my bowl!"

"Really?" said Stamp-About, wishing he hadn't been rude. "Er, I'm sorry I disturbed you. Please start all over again! But why do you have to spell each word? Why can't you just say it?"

"Don't be silly," said the little wizard. "A spell is a spell because it's spelt, isn't it? You can't make a spell unless you spell it, can you?"

"I don't know," said Stamp-About, and he came into the toadstool ring, treading on one as he did so.

"Get out!" said the wizard, pointing a long thin finger at him. "Treading on my magic toadstool! Get out! I'll turn you into a worm and call down that robin over there to eat you if you're not careful!"

Stamp-About hurriedly stepped out of the ring of toadstools, being very careful not to break one again.

"Now go away and let me start my gold spell all over again," commanded the fierce little fellow.

Stamp-About tiptoed away and hid behind a tree. All right – let the wizard order him about all he liked. He would hide and watch the spell and then he would make it too, when he got home! Aha – gold for the making – what a wonderful thing!

He peeped from behind a tree and watched. The wizard took no more notice of him. He had a pile of things to put into the glass bowl – but first he poured into it some water from a little jug.

Then he took a buttercup and shredded its golden petals one by one into the bowl, muttering as he did so.

Stamp-About strained his ears, but he couldn't catch what was being said, until he heard the wizard say, "C-U-P."

"Of course – he's only spelling the name of the flower!" thought Stamp-About. "Now – what's he putting in this time? Oh, one of the red toadstools. And now he's spelling that. Ho – what an easy spell to make!"

He watched carefully. The little wizard took another buttercup and spelt out its name, then he took a twig of hawthorn blossom and shook the white petals into the bowl and then another buttercup.

"He's spelling everything," thought Stamp-About. "Well, who would have thought that spelling had anything to do with the making of spells? This is going to be very useful to me! What is he taking now?"

The wizard had picked up the empty shell of a robin's egg and had crushed it up and dropped it into the bubbling water, which was a bright mixture of colours. He muttered as he spelt the name and then threw in yet another shower of buttercup petals. Then he danced lightly round the bowl three times and stopped.

To Stamp-About's astonishment all the water in the bowl rose up as a cloud of steam – leaving a gleaming handful of gold at the bottom of the bowl!

"Look at that," whispered Stamp-About to himself in glee, as he watched the wizard put the gold into a wallet. "Now I know exactly how to make the spell. I'll go home and do it."

The little wizard took up the bowl, put it into a small bag and then he stamped out the fire. He disappeared like a shadow through the trees.

"I'll follow him," thought Stamp-About. "He must know the way out of this wood."

So he followed carefully and soon came to a path he knew. He went one way and the little wizard went the other. Stamp-About was so excited that he went home smiling all over his face – much to the surprise of Snorty, who was leaning over his gate as Stamp-About passed.

"You're in a better temper now, are you?" called Snorty. "Well, perhaps now you'll admit that those apples of yours were bad – and that I don't owe you for them after all!"

"I don't need a penny from you, Snorty, not a penny!" said Stamp-About. "I shall soon be rich. I shall pay all the bills I owe – and you'll come borrowing from me, you see if you don't!"

Well, this was very astonishing news to Snorty, who soon spread it about that Stamp-About was going to be rich.

"How?" asked his friends. "What's he going to do? Let's go round and ask him."

When they came to Stamp-About's house he was out in his garden. He had made a small fire in the middle of the lawn, and on it he had placed a little glass bowl – the one in which his goldfish once used to swim.

"Look at that," said Snorty in amazement. "What's he doing? See – he's got a pile of strange things beside him – buttercups – a red toadstool – and what's that – the shell of an egg? And look, there's a spray of hawthorn blossom too, off the may hedge."

Stamp-About saw everyone watching and was very pleased to show off. He did exactly as he had seen the little wizard do – first he threw in the buttercup petals, shredding them off the flower head one by one. As he did so, he spelt the name out loud in a high chanting voice.

"B-u-t-t-e-r-c-u-p!"

Then he took up the red toadstool and put that into the bowl of water too. Again he chanted out loud, spelling the name clearly.

"R-e-d t-o-a-d-s-t-o-o-l!"

Then he shredded buttercup petals again and spelt the name as before, and then took the hawthorn blossom.

"H-a-w-t-h-o-r-n!"

And in went the white may petals as he shook the twig over the bowl! Aha! The water was changing colour now. Soon the handful of gold would come!

In went more buttercup petals and the name was spelt: "B-u-t-t-e-r-c-u-p!"

Then he dropped in the broken shell of a robin's egg. As he crumpled up the shell and it fell into the water, Stamp-About spelt out the name in a loud voice. "R-o-b-b-i-n's e-g-g!"

And last of all another shower of golden buttercup petals went into the bubbling water.

Eagerly Stamp-About leaned over it. Now for the gold! First the water would disappear in a cloud of steam – and then he would see the handful of gold at the bottom of the bowl!

But wait – first he must dance three times round the bowl!

Everyone crept forward to see what was about to happen. A cloud of steam shot high into the air and the water in the bowl disappeared. Then the bowl itself exploded with such a bang that everyone fell over backwards.

Stamp-About sat down very suddenly indeed, scared almost out of his wits. Then he looked eagerly at the fire – had the gold been scattered about all round it?

No – there wasn't a single piece of gold. The fire had gone out when the bowl exploded, and now only one thing lay there – a large book!

"What's happened?" shouted Stamp-About in a rage. "The spell's gone wrong! It should have made gold, not a stupid book. What book is it?"

He took it up and opened it – then he looked up in astonishment and everyone crowded round to see what it was.

"It's a dictionary!" said Snorty and he gave a huge guffaw. "Ha ha, ho ho, I'm not surprised!"

"But – why did the spell go wrong?" cried Stamp-About and he dashed the book to the ground. "I don't want a dictionary!"

"Yes, you do!" chuckled Snorty. "The spell went wrong because your spelling went wrong! Spells have to be spelled correctly! That's why all you've got is a dictionary – to help you to spell. Oh, what a joke! Can you spell 'rotten apples', Stamp-About? Oh, what a comical thing! He tried to make a spell – but he couldn't even spell!"

It was quite true. The spell couldn't work unless everything was spelled correctly and Stamp-About had conjured up something he needed as much as gold: a dictionary! Poor old Stamp-About, he hasn't paid his bills yet!